Includes Compact Disc

DISCARD

I'VE BEEN WORKING ON THE RAILROAD

Retold by STEVEN ANDERSON

Illustrated by MAXINE LEE

CANTATA
LEARNING
MANKATO, MINNESOTA

WWW.CANTATALEARNING.COM

CANTATA LEARNING
MANKATO, MINNESOTA

Published by Cantata Learning
1710 Roe Crest Drive
North Mankato, MN 56003
www.cantatalearning.com

Library of Congress Control Number: 2014957023
978-1-63290-288-7 (hardcover/CD)
978-1-63290-440-9 (paperback/CD)
978-1-63290-482-9 (paperback)

I've Been Working on the Railroad by Steven Anderson
Illustrated by Maxine Lee

Book design, Tim Palin Creative
Editorial direction, Flat Sole Studio
Executive musical production and direction, Elizabeth Draper
Music arranged and produced by Steven C Music

Printed in the United States of America.

VISIT
WWW.CANTATALEARNING.COM/ACCESS-OUR-MUSIC
TO SING ALONG TO THE SONG

A long time ago, people built **railroads**.
Trains run on railroads. They bring people
and **goods** to new places. Whoo-whoo!

Now turn the page, and sing along.

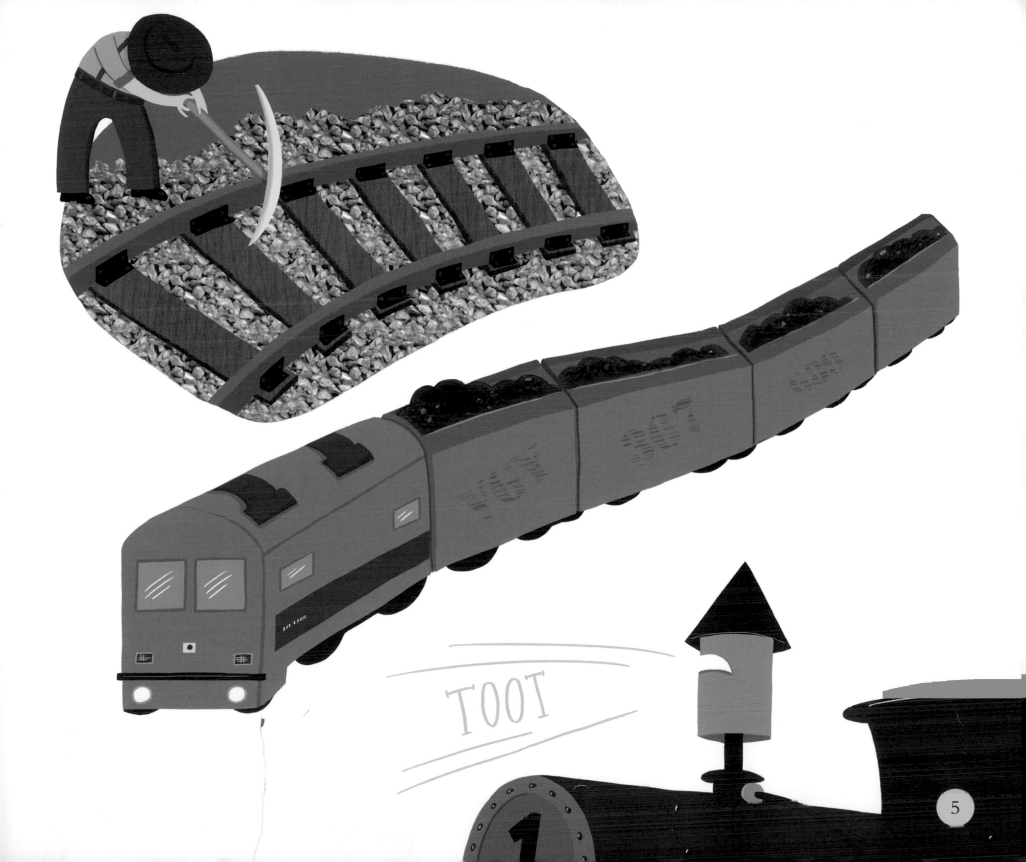

TOOT

I've been working on the railroad,

All the live long day.

I've been working on the railroad,

Just to pass the time away.

7

Don't you hear the **whistle** blowin',

Rise up so early in the **morn**?

Can't you hear the **captain** shouting,

"Dinah blow your horn!"

Dinah won't you blow, Dinah won't you blow,

Dinah won't you blow your ho-o-orn?

Dinah won't you blow, Dinah won't you blow,

Dinah won't you blow your horn?

Choo Choo

YOU HAVE FOUND A

GOLDEN TICKET

TAKE IT TO THE YOUTH DESK BY 4/30/23 TO CLAIM
A PRIZE

STAFF STAMP
HERE WHEN PRIZE
IS CLAIMED.

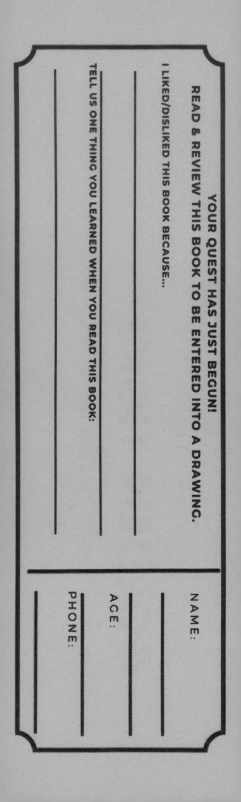

YOUR QUEST HAS JUST BEGUN!
READ & REVIEW THIS BOOK TO BE ENTERED INTO A DRAWING.

I LIKED/DISLIKED THIS BOOK BECAUSE...

_____

_____

TELL US ONE THING YOU LEARNED WHEN YOU READ THIS BOOK:

_____

NAME: _____

AGE: _____

PHONE: _____

Someone's in the kitchen with Dinah.

Someone's in the kitchen I know oh-oh.

Someone's in the kitchen with Dinah,

Strumming on the old **banjo**.

13

Fee fi fiddle e i o.

Fee fi fiddle e i o–o–o.

Fee fi fiddle e i o.

Strumming on the old banjo.

I've been working on the railroad,

All the live long day.

I've been working on the railroad,

Just to pass the time away.

Don't you hear the whistle blowin',
Rise up so early in the morn?

Can't you hear the captain shouting,
"Dinah blow your horn!"

SONG LYRICS
I've Been Working on the Railroad

I've been working on the railroad,
All the live long day.

I've been working on the railroad,
Just to pass the time away.

Don't you hear the whistle blowin',
Rise up so early in the morn?

Can't you hear the captain shouting,
"Dinah blow your horn!"

Dinah won't you blow, Dinah won't
    you blow,
Dinah won't you blow your ho-o-orn?

Dinah won't you blow, Dinah won't
    you blow,
Dinah won't you blow your horn?

Choo! Choo!

Someone's in the kitchen with Dinah.
Someone's in the kitchen I know oh-oh.

Someone's in the kitchen with Dinah,
Strumming on the old banjo.

Fee fi fiddle e i o.
Fee fi fiddle e i o-o-o.
Fee fi fiddle e i o.
Strumming on the old banjo.

I've been working on the railroad,
All the live long day.

I've been working on the railroad,
Just to pass the time away.

Don't you hear the whistle blowin',
Rise up so early in the morn?

Can't you hear the captain shouting,
"Dinah blow your horn!"

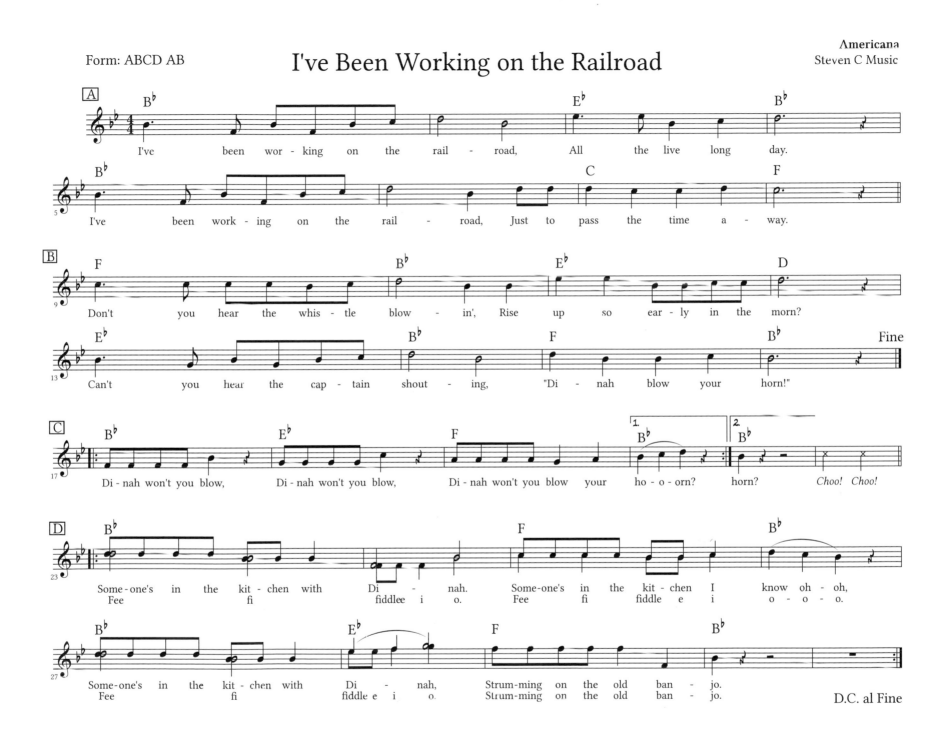

GLOSSARY

banjo—a stringed musical instrument like a guitar, but with a round body

captain—the leader of a group of people

goods—things that can be bought or sold

morn—a shorter word for morning

railroad—a set of tracks on which a train runs

whistle—an object that makes a high, loud sound

GUIDED READING ACTIVITIES

1. Where does this story take place; what is the setting? Draw or write about the setting in this story.

2. In the story, the workers want Dinah to blow the horn. What do you think this means? Why do they want Dinah to blow the horn?

3. Look through the story again. Choose one illustration. Tell a friend about it, or write about what is happening in the illustration.

TO LEARN MORE

Floca, Brian. *Locomotive*. New York: Atheneum Books for Young Readers, 2013.

Klein, Adria F. *The Full Freight Train*. Minneapolis, MN: Stone Arch Books, 2014.

Richardson, Adele D. *Freight Trains in Action*. North Mankato, MN: Capstone Press, 2012.

Sheilds, Amy. *Trains*. Washington, DC: National Geographic Children's Books, 2012.